For Ned. xxx

First published in Great Britain and in the USA in 2017 by
Otter-Barry Books, Little Orchard, Burley Gate, Herefordshire, HR1 3QS
www.otterbarrybooks.com

A catalogue record for this book is available from the British Library.

ISBN 978-1-91095-927-5

Illustrated with mixed media and collage

Printed in China

9 8 7 6 5 4 3 2 1

Monster Baby

Sarah Dyer

Otter-Barry BOOKS

Mommy says she's going
to have a baby.

Daddy says it's a good thing,
but Scamp and I aren't so sure.

Mommy needs to rest and eat **lots** of healthy food.

This means
we have to as well.

But Mommy doesn't seem to be getting any thinner.

Maybe she's resting too much.

I am a bit sad that Mommy can't carry me any more.

The hospital put jelly on
Mommy's **huge BIG** tummy,
and we saw the baby
on a screen.

I thought it looked more like a wiggly worm.

I wish the baby would come out soon, but Mommy says it won't be ready for a few more months.

Mommy says the baby can already
hear us, so I try and talk to it.

At last the baby is coming!
Granny comes to stay with us
so Daddy can take Mommy
to the hospital.

Hooray!
The baby is here at last!
I go to visit Mommy
in the hospital.

Daddy says that now
the baby monster
is here I am a
BIG monster.

I ask Scamp if
I've grown.

I **think** I'm glad to have Mommy back home, and the new baby. But I have to play quietly, even though the baby is allowed to make as much noise as he likes.

Meh meh mehh meee Wah Waah Waaaah

Lots of people come to visit
and the baby gets **LOTS** of presents.

I get some presents too, but I feel
a bit left out - and so does Scamp.

But the baby is interested in me. **Very interested!**

I think he **likes** me.

And I **think** I like him, too.

In fact, I can't wait to share
EVERYTHING
with my monster baby brother!